For Megan Howard

Reycraft Books • 55 Fifth Avenue • New York, NY 10003
Reycraftbooks.com

Reycraft Books is a trade imprint and trademark of Newmark Learning, LLC.

This edition is published by arrangement with China Children's Press & Publication Group, China.
© China Children's Press & Publication Group

Educators and Librarians: Our books may be purchased in bulk for promotional, educational, or business use. Please contact sales@reycraftbooks.com.

Library of Congress Control Number: 2020908274

ISBN: 971-1-4788-6853-8

Printed in Guangzhou, China. 4401 0520 CA22000798

10 9 8 7 6 5 4 3 2 1

First Edition Hardcover published by Reycraft Books 2020

REYCRAFT
BOOKS

Dandan's Dream

by Xiaowen Zhu

Illustrated by Yanling Gong

When the post office announced that children, in addition to letters and packages, could now be mailed, Dandan could hardly believe the news.

Many nights, Dandan had dreamed of visiting her father at the **South Pole**, where he studied icebergs. He was far away and had been gone for a long time. Now she would be able to see him!

So one day—
smash!
—Dandan broke her piggy bank and
took all her money to the post office.

"What would you like to mail?" a woman in a green uniform asked Dandan.

"ME,"

Dandan replied.
"I want to mail myself to the
South Pole to see my dad!"

The woman brought
Dandan out to the
balcony and handed her
a stack of stamps. On
each was a pair of

green wings.

"Stick these on your clothes,"
she said.

There were so many

colorful
stamps!

Dandan looked as though she
was wearing a beautiful skirt.

After Dandan stuck on the last
stamp, she felt her body grow lighter.

Gentle breezes swirled,
picked her up
off the balcony,
and whisked her
into the air.

Dandan felt as if
she were on a magical flying

She flew faster

horse.
and faster, higher and higher—

over mountains that rose like steamed buns
and green prairies that carpeted the earth.

Before long she soared above blue
seas, where too many

ships

to count floated on the water.

Suddenly, a **huge whale** lifted a big red ship from the ocean and pushed it against an island.

The ship couldn't move. Even though
the frightened crew cried for help,
the whale would not set the ship

free.

Dandan wanted to help free the ship.

But how?

The woman in the green uniform had told her how to fly, but not how to land.

Doing the only thing she could think of,
Dandan tore several stamps off herself and

dropped

them into the sea.

It worked! She flew lower.
She removed more stamps.
Down down down she went,
closer and closer to the island.

Once she had landed, Dandan raced to the shore. With all her strength, she gave the ship a powerful **push.** The whale was no match for the girl.

As the whale swam away from the newly
freed ship, the crew waved to Dandan
from the deck to thank her.

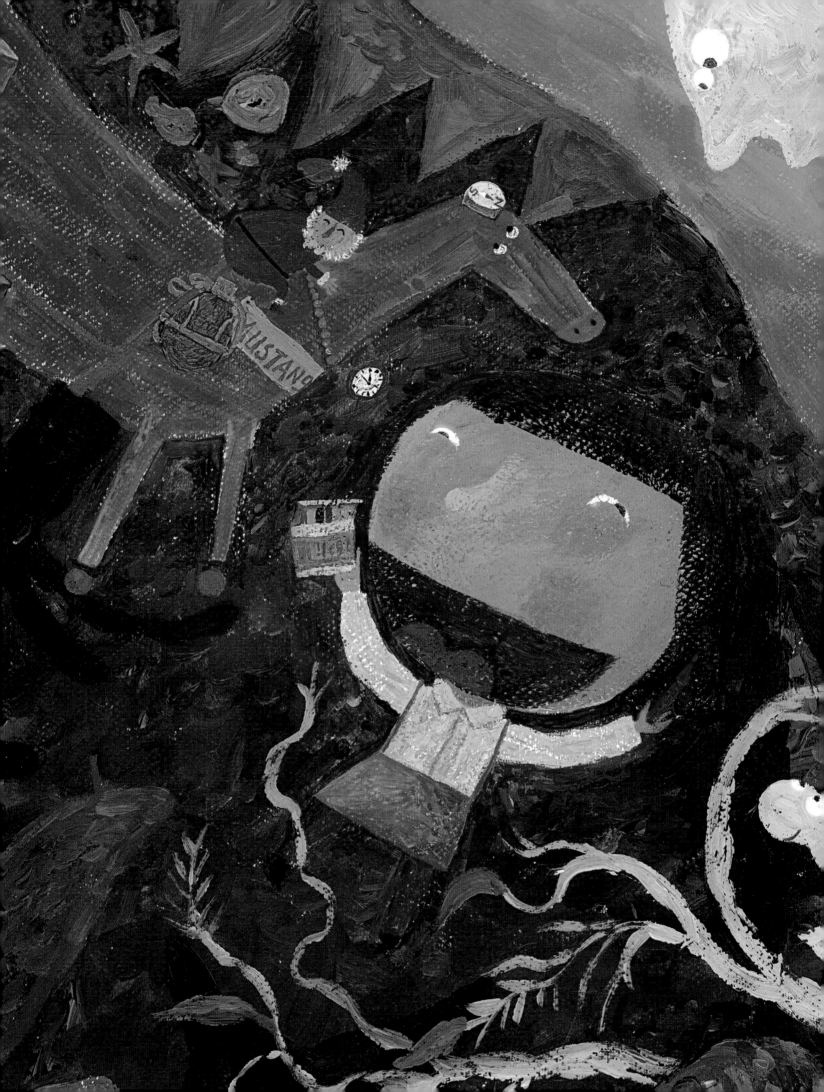

Delighted, Dandan nearly forgot she still had to mail herself to the South Pole. But where would she find stamps on an island with no people and no post office?

Dandan checked her pockets and found a box of watercolor pens. She knew just what to do!

Dandan used the pens to make her own stamps. She painted the fish she saw swimming in the sea. Then she drew a pair of large red wings.

Together, the strong red wings
flapped, lifting her out over the sea.

Soon, Dandan reached a
world of ice and snow.

The
South
Pole!

A tall man in a green coat
waved to her, surrounded
by penguins and seals.

MUSTA

"Dad!"

Dandan called out, "I'm here!

"My dream came true!"